The Other Goose

STORY AND PICTURES BY

Judith Kerr

HARPERCOLLINSPUBLISHERS

The Other Goose

Copyright © 2001 by Judith Kerr

Manufactured in China by Imago

All rights reserved.

www.harperchildrens.com

Library of Congress Cataloging-in-Publication Data

Kerr, Judith.

The other goose / Judith Kerr.

p.   cm.

Summary: Katerina the goose sees another goose in the side of Mr.
Buswell's shiny car and wishes it would come join her in the town pond.

ISBN 0-06-008254-2 — ISBN 0-06-008583-5 (lib. bdg.)

[1. Geese—Fiction.   2. Loneliness—Fiction.]   I. Title.

PZ7.K46815 Or   2002   2001039735

[E]—dc21

Typography by Jeanne Hogle

1   2   3   4   5   6   7   8   9   10

❖

First U.S. Edition, 2002

Originally published in Great Britain by HarperCollins Publishers Ltd., 2001

Once there was a goose called Katerina.

Katerina was the only goose on her pond.
There was no other goose.
This made Katerina very sad.

Sometimes Katerina thought she could see another goose.
She could see it in the side of a shiny car.
She stared and stared at it.
"One day that goose will come out," thought Katerina.
"Then I'll no longer be the only goose on the pond."

The shiny car belonged to Mr. Buswell.
Mr. Buswell looked after the bank across the road.
He said, "Just look at that silly bird.
Why do you keep staring at my car, Katerina?"

Katerina said, *"Wakwakwak!"*
Millie Buswell said nothing.
But she knew.

Everyone liked Katerina.
The baker liked her.

The lady from the toy shop liked her.

Miss Jones who taught dancing liked her

and so did Bert from the fruit shop.
They all said hello to her on their way to the bank.

At the bank Mr. Buswell looked after everyone's money.
"Take good care of it," said Bert.
Mr. Buswell said, "Just look at that silly bird.
Have you come to help me take care of the money, Katerina?"

Katerina said, *"Wakwakwak!"*
Then she went back to stare at the shiny car.

But the other goose still wouldn't come out.

One day just before Christmas, Millie Buswell said,
"We're all going to a party in the square, Katerina.
The mayor is going to switch on the Christmas lights."
Katerina said, *"Wakwakwak!"*
Then she tucked in her beak and went to sleep.

When she woke up, it was dark and she was all alone.
She thought, "I'll go and see the goose in the shiny car."
But when she looked she had a big surprise.
The car was no longer shiny and the goose had gone.

It had come out. It had come out! It had come out at last!

"Now where is it?" thought Katerina.
It was not on the pond and not on the road.

Then she saw something. Something was moving in the dark.
"*Wak!*" she shouted happily. "*Wakwakwak!*"

But it was not
the other goose.
It was a man
with a bag.

It was a big bag.
It was a
goose-sized bag
and there was
something in it.

There was a
goose-sized thing
in that goose-sized bag.

"*Wakwakwak! Wakwakwak!*" Katerina shouted very loudly.
Then she flew at the man. She nipped his hand.
She tried to nip his nose.
The man shouted, "Get off!" and ran away.

But Katerina followed him

past the shops

and down the dark streets.

She shouted and flew and tried to nip.
She wished there was someone to help her.

In the square the mayor had switched on the lights.
Suddenly there was a lot of noise. It was the noise
of a goose shouting, *"Wakwakwak! Wakwakwak!"*

"Just look at that silly bird," said Mr. Buswell.
"Katerina, what are you doing to that poor man?"
Just then the man dropped his bag.

The other goose was not in the bag after all.
"*Wak,*" said Katerina. She was very sad.
But everyone else was shouting.
"What's all this money?" shouted Mr. Buswell.

"He's robbed the bank!"
shouted the mayor.

"He's robbed *us!*"
shouted Bert.
"That's our money!"

"But Katerina
stopped him,"
said Miss Jones.

"Oh, Katerina," said Mr. Buswell, "you have saved us all.
I will never, ever again call you a silly bird."

"This brave goose should have a reward," said the mayor.
"She shall have my best buns every day," said the baker.
"And my nicest fruit," said Bert.
"We could put up a statue to her," said Miss Jones.

"Good idea," said the mayor. "Anything else?"
Millie Buswell whispered in his ear.
"Really?" said the mayor. "Are you sure?"
Millie nodded. "All right then," said the mayor.

Next day the shiny car stopped right by Katerina's pond.
And then it happened. It really happened at last.
A goose came out of the side of the shiny car.
The mayor said, "Here you are, Katerina, this is Charlie."
And Millie said, "He's going to live on the pond with you forever."

Katerina and Charlie looked at each other.

Katerina and Charlie ate grass together.

Katerina and Charlie swam on the pond together

and one day they made a nest together
and Katerina laid eggs in it.

And then there were not one, not two, not three, not four,

not five, and not six, but seven geese on Katerina's pond.

"I always knew you'd come out of
that car in the end," said Katerina.